Hot, Hot Roti for Dada-ji

BY F. ZIA   ART BY KEN MIN

LEE & LOW BOOKS · NEW YORK

LEE & LOW BOOKS Inc., 95 Madison Avenue, New York, NY 10016
leeandlow.com

Manufactured in China by Jade Productions, February 2011

Book design by ScottMylesStudios.com
Book production by The Kids at Our House

The text is set in Belwe Light and Cafeteria Bold
The illustrations are rendered in acrylic and colored pencil

10 9 8 7 6 5 4 3 2 1
First Edition

Library of Congress Cataloging-in-Publication Data
Zia, F. (Farhana)
Hot, hot roti for Dada-ji / by F. Zia ; art by Ken Min. — 1st ed.
p. cm.
Summary: Aneel and his grandfather, Dada-ji, tell stories, use their
imaginations, and make delicious roti, a traditional Indian flatbread.
ISBN 978-1-60060-443-0 (hardcover : alk. paper)
[1. Grandfathers—Fiction. 2. East Indian Americans—Fiction.] I. Min, Ken, ill. II. Title.
PZ7.Z482Ho 2011
[E]—dc22   2010034694

For Aydin, Samar, and Gabriella, and for S.M.Z.,
Ann Behar, and Jennifer Fox . . . with gratitude
–F.Z.

For Mom, who makes the best meals for me.
And a tip of the hat to my Busters/Tanners Crew
for all their support
–K.M.

Aneel was glad his grandparents had come to stay. Dada-ji was teaching him to stand on his head and to sit like a serene lotus. Dadi-ma's prayer song made him bob his head from side to side, and the sweet, curling smoke from her incense stick tickled his nose so!

But his grandparents' stories were the best of all. Aneel loved hearing about the faraway village with the green wheat fields and the swaying coconut palms.

"Who's telling me a story?" asked Aneel one day. No one answered. Sweet smoke snaked into his nose, and the tinkle of a tiny bell murmured in his ear.

Dadi-ma's eyes were closed. "*Hari Om, Hari Om,*" she chanted.

Aneel turned to Dada-ji, who was standing on his head.
"Will you tell me a story, Dada-ji?" Aneel asked.
"*Hunh-ji*, yes, sir, one minute," said upside-down Dada-ji. Then he flipped over, landing with a soft *THUP*, and became a serene lotus on the rug.
Aneel hopped on his grandfather's lotus lap, and Dada-ji began.

In a village far, far away where the warm breeze made the green wheat fields dance and the brown coconuts rustle lived a lad who astonished the villagers morning, noon, and night.

Aneel winked at Dada-ji. After all, the lad in the story was none other than his very own Dada-ji long, long ago. Dada-ji went on . . .

In the morning the lad wrestled a snorting water buffalo, and the villagers cried,
"Arre Wah! oh wow!"

At noon he tied two hissing cobras in a knot. "Wah!" cheered the villagers.

At night the mighty lad spun three trumpeting elephants by their tails. **"Wah! Wah!"** shouted the villagers.

What made the lad so strong? It was the hot, hot roti that sizzled and wizzled on *Badi-ma*'s wood hearth. You see, *baba*, Badi-ma made the best roti around! Hungry villagers trampled tall fields and swam angry rivers to sniff the fluffy-puffy roti that bubbled and wobbled in *ghee* on the hot, hot *tavva* pan.

Each day the lucky lad smacked his lips and rubbed his belly and ate a stack so high with a bit of tongue-burning mango pickle. He wanted the power of the tiger, baba!

After the lad had gobbled up the last roti, he licked salty specks from his fingertips one by one and burped twice–*uur, uur*. Then the power came rolling in like a great flood.

"ARRE WAH!"

"Hunh-ji! Yes, sir!" said the mighty lad. And off he went to do more wonderful things.

He made the earth rumble beneath him in the morning.

He shook the giant mango tree for Badi-ma's pickle pot at noon.

And he touched the blue, blue sky
with his bare feet at night.

"Arre Wah!" the villagers roared.

"Wah! Wah!"

Dada-ji looked at Aneel and rubbed his belly. A rumble grew into a mighty roar. He smacked his lips.

"Does the lad still have the power, Dada-ji?" Aneel asked.

"There's only one way to find out, baba," said his grandfather.

"Does he want roti today?" Aneel asked.

"Hunh-ji. Hot, hot roti," Dada-ji said, his mouth beginning to water.

"With salty grains to lick?" said Aneel.

". . . and a bit of tongue-burning mango pickle!" Dada-ji said, drooling a little.

Aneel ran to ask his mother to make roti, but she was on the phone with Auntie Veenu.

So Aneel tugged at the edge of Dadi-ma's sari. "No roti today," she said with her eyes and shooed him away.

Next Aneel tried his dad, who only ruffled the newspaper and dug his nose deeper into the pages.

Finally Aneel tried his big sister, Kiran, but she didn't want sticky globs of dough getting under her starry nails.

"Don't worry, Dada-ji," said Aneel. "I watch Mom make roti all the time. I'll help you get your power back."

Aneel opened the kitchen cupboard. He pushed past the rice and the red lentils. He pushed past the spices and the green lentils. "Watch out!" cried Mom.

Aneel found the flour and dumped some into a big bowl.
Aneel found the salt and dumped that in too.
"*Ai hai!* Oh dear!" exclaimed Dadi-ma. "So much?"
But Dada-ji loved salt.
Next Aneel added the water.
"Tch! Tch!" cried Mom. "So much?"

Kiran laughed at the watery mess, but Aneel
didn't care. He just dumped in more flour.
AACHOO! Kiran sneezed in a floury cloud.
"Arre wah! The boy has talent," cried Dada-ji.

Aneel mixed the flour and water

and added more salt

and began to knead the dough.

He punched . . .

and he pushed . . .

and he pulled.

"Arre wah! Exactly like Badi-ma," shouted Dada-ji.

When the dough was smooth, Aneel rolled it into balls—
enough for a roti stack as high as the ceiling.

Then Aneel grabbed a rolling pin and one of the balls. The dough stuck here and it stuck there, but Aneel didn't give up. He rolled north, and he rolled south. He rolled east, and he rolled west.

"Hunh-ji!" cheered Dada-ji. "Here it goes!"

Bit by little bit the first roti began to form.

"It looks like the U.S.A!" Kiran said, and laughed.

"Roti can be any shape, right, baba?" Dada-ji said, winking at Aneel.

Aneel rolled out more and more balls of roti dough.

"*Dekho!* Look! Roti number ten is a perfect circle," remarked Dadi-ma.

"Hunh-ji. Practice makes perfect," said Dada-ji.

When it was time to cook the roti, Dadi-ma got the tavva pan smoky hot and added some butter. The first roti hissed. Very carefully, Dadi-ma helped Aneel flip it. The roti danced and sputtered some more, all brown and buttery.

"Did Badi-ma make them like this?" Aneel asked.

"Hunh-ji!" Dada-ji said, nodding.

At last all the roti were ready.
Aneel piled them up in a high,
high stack.
"Hot, hot roti for Dada-ji!"
he announced in his biggest voice.

"Wah! Wah!" exclaimed Dada-ji. He grabbed a warm, steamy roti from the stack and took one bite . . . and another . . . and another. He chomped and he chewed.

Mmmmm! Mmmmm! Dada-ji said, smacking his lips.

Sluuurp! Sluuurp! Sluuurp! He licked salty specks from his fingertips one by one.

"Do you feel the power, Dada-ji?" Aneel asked.

"Hunh-ji!" Dada-ji said, flexing his muscles. "Find me a snorting water buffalo to wrestle!"

Aneel giggled. "There are no water buffalo here."

"Two hissing cobras to tie in a knot?" Dada-ji asked.

"Dada-ji!" Aneel laughed.

"Well, surely those are three elephants I hear trumpeting in the backyard," Dada-ji said as he gobbled up another roti and licked the salt from his fingertips. "Anything is possible, baba. Let's see what we can do."

Hand in hand, Aneel and Dada-ji went outside to find new adventures.

First they made the earth rumble under their feet.

Then they shook a mighty apple tree for Dadi-ma's pie.

Last, they made bare feet touch
the blue, blue sky.

"Dada-ji, the power came back!" Aneel cried.
Dada-ji smiled. "Hunh-ji!" he said. "The power of
the hot, hot roti came back to the lad from a village
far, far away. Thank you, my tiger. Thank you!"

Glossary

Pronunciations for Hindi words are approximations for English speakers.
Hindi is a language spoken widely in India. All syllables in Hindi are stressed equally.

ai hai (eye hi): oh dear

arre wah (are wah): ah wow

baba (ba-ba): dear child, term of affection similar to "buddy"

badi-ma (buh-dee-ma): great-grandmother

dada-ji (da-da-jee): paternal grandfather (father's father)

dadi-ma (da-dee-mah): paternal grandmother (father's mother)

dekho (deck-ho *or* day-kho): look

ghee (ghi): a type of butter used in Indian cooking

hari om (hah-ree ohm): chant recited to clear the mind

hunh-ji (hun-jee): yes, sir

roti (roh-tee): flat, unleavened bread made from whole wheat flour

sari (sah-ree): dresslike garment of wrapped cloth worn by women of India

tavva (tah-va): flat pan used in Indian cooking

wah (wah): wow